Odell T. Fellows

Rhymes of Reform

BY

ODELL T. FELLOWS

PRESS OF
GEO. A. SWERDFIGER
PASADENA, CAL.

ᴴ

TO

My Mother,

SARAH PALMER WELD,

KENDUSKEAG, MAINE.

PREFACE.

Not all of the contents of this little booklet can properly be called Reform Poems, but it is thought that a sufficient number of them are of that order to warrant the title. It is the author's first venture, and is offered to the public without apology, in the full conviction that it will meet with only the reception which it merits, and nothing more is desired. Should the result be anywise encouraging, it will no doubt be followed by others from the same source.

O. T. F.

Pasadena, Cal., 1897.

INDEX.

MOTHER'S OLD WHEEL.

Alone in my bachelor quarters
  I wait for the coming of night:
The walls of my "den" are gilded,
  The fire on my hearth is bright.
Success in the world of traffic,
  Has crowned my tireless zeal;
But I hear to-night in the twilight
  The sound of mother's old wheel.

Oh, many the days and years,
  Since this weary race begun!
And with many a twist, the thread
  Of my life is nearly spun.
Success is a failure mostly,
  Then blame me not if I feel
That I hear in the winds at twilight
  The sound of mother's old wheel.

On the well-worn floor of the kitchen
  It stood in the long ago,
And the patient feet of the spinner
  Walked ever to and fro.
And now as the gathering shadows
  Around my casement steal;
There's a wail in the winds of evening
  That sounds like mother's old wheel.

MOTHER'S OLD WHEEL.

Oh, the threads of our lives are tangled
  And twisted in many a knot!
But how far soever they lead us,
  There's ever a dearest spot.
And the place and the sound I'll remember
  Till I pass to the land of the leal,
Are the old kitchen floor of my childhood
  And the sound of mother's old wheel.

TURN ON THE LIGHT.

Turn on the light!
Unto the world's awakened sight,
Reveal the glorious heritage
That may be ours, if we but dare
To leave the past, the outgrown age;
Turn to the future's virgin page,
Inscribe the one word "Progress" there,
And, standing forth in manhood's might,
Turn on the light.

Turn on the light!
They shun it not who love the right;
But wrong and error flee away,
And hide from out its living rays
As evil things forsake the day,
And, in their dark and devious ways,
Their mischief plot.   But all shall praise
Brave souls, who, in the strength of right,
Turn on the light.

Turn on the light!
Though envious greed, in sore affright,
Shall tremble in her place of power;
And vainly grasp the useless hoard
Of ill-got wealth.   This very hour

TURN ON THE LIGHT.

I see the threatening storm-cloud lower
Where bread for hungry men is stored,
And law but mocks them in their plight—
    Turn on the light.

    Turn on the light!
Ere darkness settles into night!
    Let not Columbia's hallowed soil,
That holds the dust of Washington
    Who fought to free the sons of toil,
    His name forgot, his fame despoil,
A deathless fame so nobly won!
In his dear name, in Heaven's sight,
    Turn on the light.

THE PRESENT HOUR.

This is the hour that's big with fate,
And while our hearts expectant wait
  Within the hush before the storm,
  We nurse our hope to keep it warm,—
Our hope, well-nigh disconsolate.

O darkening skies of Freedom's land,
Be ours thy fury to command!
  Why this foreboding in the soul
  That we may view thy tempests roll
By lightning flash and blazing brand?

And was it this for which they fought,
Who counted life as less than naught
  When human rights were trampled down?
  And unto him who wore the crown
Said "See, oh, see thou do it not!"

Be wise in time, O ye who take
From Labor's meed; or ye may wake
  To hear from huts where sorrows dwell
  With rising power the chorus swell:
"Yet once again for Freedom's sake!"

RUTHLESS TIME.

Now time again is at its flood,
And great events come trooping past
Like maskers at a carnival;
And some we see in friendly guise
And some in masks of grief and loss,
Whose other names are joy and gain;
And dire misfortune, which we dread,
Like visits of the angel Death.

Along the shore lies strewn the wrecks
Of shattered hopes, that, putting forth
In morning's prime, essayed in vain
To ride upon tempestuous seas
Without a firm and practiced hand
To guide their bark among the shoals
Of life, where sunken rocks lay thick,
With jaws as cruel as death itself.

So time flows on.   With ruthless hand
The shrinking soul is thrust aside,
As down the teeming ways of life
The multitude still hurries on.
And other barks are putting forth
Upon the voyage untried, unknown,
And they shall suffer shipwreck, too;
And thus till time shall be no more.

SONS OF THE MORNING.

O sons of the morning, awake!
Heard ye not the loud call to the fray?
The forms of oppression, the slayers of right,
That have lurked in the shadows and gloom of the night,
They surely are passing away.

O sons of the morning, arise!
The sky is resplendent in hue.
Where the fields have been sown by the wisdom of years
And watered and kept by humanity's tears,
The harvest is waiting for you.

Brave sons of the morning, we wait.
And hope lives within us again,
That justice shall rise from the gloom of the past
And the soul of the people be lifted at last
From out of its travail and pain.

Glad sons of the morning, take heart,
Your words they are with us today,
And they fill us with hope and with courage to fight,
Till the hosts of oppression, the foes of the right,
Shall be conquered forever and aye.

11

SONS OF THE MORNING.

And then, O ye glorious sons
Of a day that is dawning at last!
Shall we bask in the light of fraternity's ray,
And the nightmare of poverty vanish away
Like a hideous dream that is past?

I MAY BE WRONG.

It seems to me the day is long
    Since politicians tried to do,
When they were sent to make the laws,
    One-half the things they promised to.
But when it comes to making "stuff,"
    They work together good and strong,
And get themselves fixed well enough;
    But then, of course, I may be wrong.

I can't help thinking, right or wrong,
    It's a disgrace, a lasting shame,
When legislators play the thief,
    And call themselves another name.
A people outraged and betrayed
    Should make them sing a sadder song;
Could they be stripped and whipped and flayed
    It might not be so very wrong.

But be it so, I'll sing my song,
    And pray the day may swiftly come
When those who serve themselves alone,
    We shall elect to stay at home.
When men and patriots, true and tried,
    The halls of state shall thickly throng,
But while I pray, and hope beside,
    I may be wrong, I may be wrong.

THE CAPTAIN AND MATE.

It was night on the deep, and the waters reposed
Like the unquiet sleeper; faint stars were disclosed
By the rifts in the clouds which had gathered around,
And the silence of midnight was deep and profound.

All idly and purposeless drifted my bark
On the face of the waters so dreary and dark;
The fitful winds fanned me and bore me away,
While I waited and watched for the coming of day.

But now on my listening ear, faintly and sweet,
Fell the sound of an oar with its rythmical beat;
And I saw through the gloom, with her colors on high,
A fair goodly ship that was passing me by.

Bearing straight on her course like the dread ship of fate,
At her prow, side by side, stood the Captain and Mate;
And I eagerly hailed from my fullness of heart,
For I was drifting alone, without rudder or chart.

Would they hear? Would they heed? Would they come
        to my side?
Or leave me to drift on the waters so wide?
I could only call loudly and breathlessly wait
Till the answer came back from the Captain and Mate.

14

THE CAPTAIN AND MATE.

And it came; and with song and with answering shout
The ship, in the darkness of night, put about,
And came to my side in response to my hail,
And the Captain and Mate clasped my hand o'er the rail.

And I said: "Where away through the gloom and the
     night?
Is the haven ahead?   Is the harbor in sight?
Is there land in the distance? Oh, tell me I pray,
Is the night nearly gone? Is there sign of the day?"

Then they answered me calmly: "The night speeds away;
We behold in the east the faint flush of the day.
We have come from the west where the shadows are born,
And we sail to the east, to the land of the morn."

They were off and away toward the dim distant land,
And I, seizing an oar with a resolute hand,
Followed fast in their wake with a confident stroke,
Until soon, o'er the waters, the rising day broke.

And we entered the harbor, and soft was the breeze,
And before was the land with its flowers and trees,
With the songs of sweet birds and music of rills,
And the bluest of skies o'er the greenest of hills.

Now the anchor I cast in the harbor of rest,
In the sight of the land, the bright land of the blest;
No longer to drift, or to hopelessly wait,
For I'm guided to port by the Captain and Mate.

CONSCIENCE'S VOICE.

Like the water's rythmic flow
Underneath the ice and snow,
Conscience's voice doth whisper low.

'Tis the power that in us lies
From the old estate to rise,
Phoenix-like to fairer skies.

By this light that burns within,
Seek each soul-destroying sin—
Self-approval seek to win.

Not by dragging others down
Shall we gain the victor's crown,
Rich reward or great renown.

Not by stalking through the land
With iconoclastic hand,
Smiting all the shrines that stand.

But by love we bear the new,
By the god-like will to do;
Cherishing the good and true.

By the light that gilds the skies,
Brighter where our pathway lies,
By the faith that never dies.

HENRY GEORGE.

Upon his bed in painless sleep
   He resteth now, he resteth well,
While grateful hearts his memory keep
   And loving lips his praises tell.

So well he strove for truth and right,
   For justice to the toiling one,
That, though his face be lost to sight,
   His words shall live till time is done.

No despot, seated on the throne,
   But blanched with fear to hear his voice;
He bade the wrong be overthrown;
   He bade the hopeless one rejoice.

For right, he said, should win the day,
   Though long delayed by selfish greed;
The good time, once so far away,
   Since he has lived, is near, indeed.

So at the front he bravely fell;
   Oh, glorious fate! Oh, happy lot!
'Tis well, ye struggling ones, 'tis well!
   For Henry George is not forgot.

PASADENA.

Pasadena! have you seen her,
    Fairest maid beneath the sun?
With the sea of bloom about her,
    Where the tides of summer run?

Waves of perfume and of color
    Roll upon the magic strand;
While the mountains, grim and stately,
    As a guard around her stand.

Pasadena! I have seen her
    With the glory on her brow,
And the vision of her splendor
    Lingers in my memory now.

With the light of joy around her,
    With a smile upon her face,
Bearing balm of health and healing
    For the children of the race.

Fairer palaces than ever
    Graced the hills of classic Greece,
Testify to grand achievements
    In the arts of love and peace.

PASADENA.

Fountains play in shady bowers,
 Fruits hang ripening in the sun,
Whispering leaves and smiling flowers
 Welcome speak to every one.

Not the poor and not the needy
 In those bowers of beauty dream;
Nay, there are no poor and needy
 In this city of my dream.

All the want and all the sorrow
 That our hearts congeal today,
In the warmth of love fraternal,
 Have forever passed away.

Oh, for words to paint it truly!
 Oh, for painter's brush to limn!
Ere the vision fade forever
 From my memory faint and dim.

And I see arise before me
 Pictures full of shame and dread,
Where, within a land of plenty,
 Men and women want for bread.

Build, O brothers, firm and lasting,
 Build beside the living stream,
Build upon the rock of ages,
 Build the city of my dream!

PASADENA.

Let me see its towers arising
  Where the plain and mountain and meet;
Singing grove and peaceful grotto
  Haste, Oh hasten to complete!

For the world is sick with waiting;
  Brothers perish day by day;
Build, Oh build the promised city,
  Do not, do not long delay!

Let mine eyes behold the glory
  Of this earthly paradise;
They will gladly close forever
  When that blessed morn shall rise.

MY WINDOW.

When care weighs down my troubled soul,
  I seek this sheltered seat,
"When passions wild brook no control,"
  Let this be my retreat.

Perhaps a memory clings around
  This spot so strangely dear,
Perhaps I hold it hallowed ground
  For those who've lingered here.

Roll, queenly Moon, more softly roll,
  Above this holy place;
Beam calmly on this troubled soul,
  I love thy pitying face.

Hast thou not seen what other eyes
  Will never, never see?
Hast thou not seen, in mortal guise,
  An angel here with me?

Hast thou not seen, but lisp it not,
  While countless seasons run,
"Two souls with but a single thought,
  Two hearts that beat as one?"

21

CHRISTMAS GREETINGS

From the land of flowers with hand and heart,
 I greet you, friend, this Christmas night.
Though fate decreed that we should part,
Your face from out the past will start
 To keep your memory ever bright.

By the cheerful hearthfire's ruddy glow
 I see you sit in glowing light.
Under the boughs of mistletoe,
Where laughing faces come and go,
 Yours I see, this Christmas night.

Mine the path in sunnier climes,
 Beneath the skies of sunset light;
But still I hear the merry chimes,
And think of friends of those old times,
 And wish them joy this Christmas night.

WHEN WE MEET AGAIN.

Last night I looked from out my door,
  The slumbrous moon was past its full;
Strange shapes of clouds sailed slow before,
  Like voyaging ships, with sail and hull
Distinct outlined on night's broad sea,
  And somehow, cloud and moon and sky,
With subtle charm brought back to me
  Another night long since gone by.

The old year languished; calm and still
  The orange groves in fragrance slept;
The moon had climbed the distant hill
  And o'er the world its radiance swept.
The lights shone out from windows near,
  The stars came forth from heaven afar,
But what, to eyes that beamed so clear,
  Were flickering lamp or twinkling star?

O night, sweet night, without the glare
  And dust of noon, or busy strife!
When cool winds fan the brow of care,
  And grace and beauty hallow life.
Pass not, sweet hour, too swiftly by,
  But may we find surcease of pain,
And gaze upon that moon and sky
  When, soul to soul, we meet again.

THE SONG FROM THE CASEMENT.

I listened and lingered long
  To a sound that floated afar,
To the sad, sweet words of a song
  And the notes of a throbbing guitar.

Till the tremulous chords had died
  On the evening drear and chill;
Till the last faint echo replied,
  And all was solemn and still.

But the ravishing strains I heard
  Are echoing still in my soul;
Sweeter than song of a bird
  Burst forth beyond control.

Oh, singer with voice divine!
  Your song, it was not for me;
But I praise you, the song is mine,
  Whoever, wherever you be.

In the evening drear sing out,—
  In the night through dark and rain;
Some soul in the gloom without
  Shall hear that heavenly strain.

For never a song was sung
  But formed of the life a part.
No matter how winning the tongue,
  'Tis the song that reaches the heart.

GUARDIAN.

She found me wandering lone and far,
　When day was late and winds were chill.
When frowning skies revealed no star
　To guide my steps o'er bare bleak hill,
Or wind-swept plain, where bush and scaur
　My terrors mocked with echoes shrill.

I heard the distant ocean roar
In endless grief on its wild shore,
　And o'er my head, fierce birds of prey,
　With hoarse cries, mourned the dying day;
When lo! she came, the radiant one,
　With smiles of morning on her face,
And, like the glorious risen sun,
　Her presence lighted all the place.

The shadows fled, the new light broke,
From doubt and fear my soul awoke;
No more dismayed by frowning skies,
Or sea-birds harsh, discordant cries,
　For as the wind of morning blows
From out the east new glories rise.
　But never stars in heaven rose
That matched the splendor of her eyes,

And since one word from those sweet lips,
I fear no more night's dark eclipse.

Though winds may rave and oceans roar,
Though stars may set to rise no more,
　The ways we tread through seeming night
　Are but as pathways toward the light.

No shore so lone, no land so drear,
But guardian ones are hovering near;
　No gloom so deep, no plain so wide,
　That man from his own soul may hide.

Look up, sad one, when fears dismay,
　When naught but gloom around thee lies!
It is thy great, thy glorious day,
　When o'er its ills thy soul may rise.

'Twas given thee to suffer long,
　But grand the meed by suffering brought;
To rise triumphant over wrong,
　And reach the goal which thou hast sought.

ANNIVERSARY OF THE ROCHESTER KNOCKINGS.

Once again the rolling season
  Brings the promise of the spring;
Once again, beneath the starlight,
  Do we hear the angels sing,
As they sang in days departed
  Heralding the Savior's birth,
So, tonight, in joy proclaiming
  Many saviors to the earth.

Saving from the sin and sorrow,
  From the woe of blindness born,
Leading souls from out the darkness,
  Guiding to the glorious morn.
Lo! it breaks, the day of promise,
  Higher mounts the sun of truth,
And the soul of man, awaking,
  Revels in eternal youth.

Long the night of watching, waiting,
  For a symbol or a sign
From the land of the immortals,
  From the spheres of life divine.
And it came; the hour propitious,
  Fate no longer could defer;
'Twas the timid knock that sounded
  In that home in Rochester.

Faintly knocking at the portal
    Of the crumbling house of clay,
Knocking till the stone of error
    From the tomb is rolled away;
And the Lord of Life arising
    Walks in beauty forth again,
Bearing *proofs* of life immortal
    To the waiting sons of men.

Want and sorrow, clothed in tatters,
    Crouch and wait beside our door:
Sin and suffering, boon companions,
    Haunt the dwellings of the poor.
But the dawn of hope draws nearer
    For the outcast and forlorn;
Doubt no more enshrouds the future,
    On this day the truth was born.

Through the ways of doubt and error
    Groped we in the misty past,
Hoping, struggling and despairing,
    'Mong the shadows deep and vast;
Baffled by the hordes of evil,
    Overthrown by wrong and ill,
Yet o'er all the god-like spirit
    Rises, and is living still.

Living to subdue and conquer
    Every vile, unworthy thing,
Every thought that, born of evil,
    Lifts its head to strike and sting;

Crush it out, the selfish motive,
　'Neath the heel of self-control;
Straitway build upon the ruins,
　Fairer structures for the soul.

Hark! that knock tonight is sounding,
　Knocking, knocking, yet again,
Seeking to reveal the message
　Long withheld from dying men;
Dying in anticipation
　Of a night of endless gloom,
Seeing not the hope that glimmers
　Through the darkness of the tomb.

But that knock has come to waken
　From the sleep of ages past,
And we enter at the doorway
　Of the house of God at last.
As we wait within the portal
　We behold the dawning light
Faintly shining through the curtain
　Of the temple of the night.

Lo! the night is nearly ended,
　Day has set his seal on high;
Broader grows the flush of crimson
　Over all the future's sky.
Superstition, wrong and error
　Flee before the rising morn,
Nature wakes to join the chorus,
　On this day the truth was born.

YOUTH, HEALTH AND LOVE.

In rosy morn from out my door I gazed,
   And lo! I saw a path all strewn with flowers;
And said, with swelling heart, "now God be praised,
   The fairest way in this fair world of ours
Is mine to tread. No sorrow lurks beside;
   But on I'll go from golden day to day,
With Youth, and Health, and Love, my willing bride,
   And fairer scenes shall open all the way."

We sallied forth. The day was young and bright;
   Sweet youth went with us up the first ascent;
We bravely toiled, but thorns, concealed from sight,
   Did pierce our feet and hands as on we went.
Then Youth forsook me, ever fickle Youth!
   But what cared I since Health and Love remained ?
I waved good-by, and said, which was the truth,
   That I had lost far less than I had gained.

But now the path, devoid of flowers or shade,
   Led through the glare and dust of busy marts,
Where clanging hoofs and grinding wheels of trade
   Drive ever over quivering human hearts;
Or through dim halls, where, motionless and pale,
   Like statues sit, from weary day to day,
The sons of toil; here Health began to fail,
   And drooped and died, and dropped beside the way.

YOUTH, HEALTH AND LOVE.

But Love remains through dark vicissitude,
  And murmurs not, though Youth and Health are gone.
The hour grows late, the winds are cold and rude,
  The sky o'ercast, but still we journey on.
No accident can e'er our progress stay;
  We were, we are, and we shall ever be.
Though Youth and Health and all may pass away,
  Our path leads on throughout eternity.

DAY-DREAMS.

We have dreamed of fame and glory,
    We have dreamed of feats sublime;
And wished a name to live in story,
    Sounding down the aisles of time.

We have fought the fight of anguish,
    We have battled long with sin;
Many foes without, we've vanquished,
    And a mightier foe within.

All of life is incompleteness;
    All of youth has passed away;
Precious few the drops of sweetness
    We have found beside the way.

Now and then the sunbeams straying,
    All the joys of heaven bring;
Here and there a fount is playing,
    Here and there the sweet birds sing.

We may say in aimless living
    That we bow to God's behest.
We may tire of constant striving,
    We may find no place of rest.

32

DAY-DREAMS.

Yet a dream we ever cherish,
    That beyond this vale of tears,
Waits a beauty that shall perish
    Nevermore, through all the years.

Courage take for great endeavor,
    Doubt it not, this truth sublime,
That throughout the long forever
    Stretch the heights that we must climb.

MORNING, NOON AND NIGHT.

When morning comes to deck the east
  With brightening hues of red and gold;
When, like one bidden to the feast,
  I see new glories quick unfold;
    The rising day to me is sweet,
    For at its close we two shall meet.

When noon is high o'er all the land—
  The joyous land of bud and bloom;
When flowers smile on every hand
  To banish all my thoughts of gloom;
    As turns the flower unto the sun,
    I turn to you, my chosen one.

When evening shadows gather near
  And wild birds seek the sheltering tree:
When in the skies the stars appear
  To tell their tales of constancy,
    No stars I need to light my skies
    For light that beams from your dear eyes.

When comes the night of holy calm,
  With thoughts of you my dreams are blest;
And in that land of sleep and balm
  My head is pillowed on your breast:—
    I start and wake; dark night I see,
    Until you smile again on me.

THE JOURNEY OF LIFE.

Through a land that was beautiful, smiling and glad,
Once methought I was journeying, lonely and sad;
For the way that I travelled, oh, sad is the tale!
Had a wall on each side which I never could scale.

And as weary I walked in the dust and the heat,
I could see on the hillside a shady retreat;
But my feet could not stray, although great was my need,
And the pain of my journey seemed bitter indeed.

For my brain was afire with the heat and the thirst
And the veins of my temples seemed ready to burst,
I had wandered so far, I had suffered it all
For the things that now mocked me, just over the wall.

There were flowers and bowers, and fruit of the vine
And the peoples' glad song as they pressed out the wine;
There was gold of the orange and bloom of the peach
To tempt me and taunt me, just out of my reach.

Some would pause in their work in those gardens so fair,
And would carelessly cast on the traveller there
A kind look of compassion, of pity I thought,
And a word to encourage, my straining ear caught.

THE JOURNEY OF LIFE.

Oh, 'twas hard, in the sight of those bowers of bliss,
To be toiling along on a journey like this;
Far behind was but sorrow, and joy that was dead,
Far away in the future the dreary way led.

Had I heard not the songs of the singers that wrought,
Had I never a sound of their loving words caught,
Had I seen not the flowers and fruitage so rare
I had known not the pangs of a hopeless despair.

'Tis the sight of the gladness while walking in gloom,
'Tis the beauty that borders the path to the tomb,
Casts the shadow that falls o'er the terrible strife
Where the soul is athirst for the waters of life.

'Tis, O mortal wayfarer, no fancy I see,—
'Tis a journey that's travelled by you and by me:
In the sight of the joys that our spirits would share
Do we grope in the dust and the gloom of despair.

Do we trust at the end there is rest for the soul?
'Tis a hope that enlivens and brightens the whole.
It is all that we have, 'tis our refuge in need,
For deprive us of this and we perish indeed.

THE LOVELY DEAD.

The form of grace, the sparkling eye,
  The heart that beat with pleasure;
Fell fate decreed that she should die,
  Our child, our countless treasure.

The fairest gem vouchsafed to earth
  Returned to God the keeper;
No song of joy, no sound of mirth
  Can wake the lovely sleeper.

The saddened home, the sacred tomb,
  The shadows lifted never,
A darker night, a deeper gloom
  Is on my soul forever.

THE DAY'S ADVANCE.

Where the wild Atlantic surges beat the cliffs of 'Quoddy
    Head,
  O'er the ocean dim and distant first appeared the rising
    day;
Then the mists, dispersed and scattered by the shafts the
    morning shed,
  Fled along the sounding headlands toward the isles of
    Casco Bay.

Over inland, hill and river, to the far Aroostook wild,
  Flashed the message of the morning, "Lo the day is
    born again!"
Streamlets laughed, and lakes of silver in the face of
    heaven smiled,
  While the pine-tree and the hemlock whispered back
    the glad refrain.

Up the stretches of Penobscot, past the Indian's cabin
    lone,
  From the brows of old Katahdin gleamed the light of
    glorious day,
And from Moosehead's mighty waters rose the mists of
    morning, blown
  Toward the riotous Androscoggin thundering down
    his rocky way.

Westward still the hosts of morning, speeding on the
  wings of light,
  Enter not the slumbering forest where the shades are
  dark and deep,
But they climb with noiseless footsteps o'er the mountain's dizzy height,
  Leap across the smiling valleys with a grand, majestic
  sweep.

O'er the lordly Hudson flashing, soon to leave it far
  behind,
  Then to span Niagara's chasm with a crescent many-
  hued;
Over inland sea and prairie, faster than the truant
  wind,
  Is the march of day triumphant through the desert
  solitude.

Tarry not, O bright Evangel, in those deserts lone and
  bare,
  Bring the message to thy children on the far Pacific's
  shore;
We behold thy signs appearing through the night of
  our despair,
  And we watch thy glorious coming as we never watch-
  before.

We are brothers—we are brothers of the stalwart sons
  of Maine,—
  We would clasp our hands in concord o'er the nation
  of our dreams,
With no lord upon her highway and no serf upon her
  plain,
  When the golden gate is closing on the day's departing
  beams.

DINNER.

O, sweetest sound that greets the ear!
The fire bell striking loud and clear,
And hurried tramp of horses' feet
In the engine house across the street;
O, blessed hour for one and all
To hear the cook's inviting call:
            "Dinner!"

Within that mansion grand and lone,
Where Want, the spectre, is not known;
Where silver plate and mirror blaze
With many a light's reflected rays,
At day's decline they gather round
In answer to that magic sound:
            "Dinner!"

By dusty road, by iron rail,
Beside the desert's dreary trail,
In shady bower, by farm-yard gate,
The weary hobos congregate
To share what luck may chance to bring
For their repast, and call the thing
            "Dinner!"

O, ye who dine from costly plate,
Scorn not your brother at the gate;
Throughout a life of selfish ease
What have ye done for such as these?

DINNER.

Do ye, when shades of evening fall,
Extend to them the welcome call:
      "Dinner ?"

Then prate no more of Christian faith,
Nor build your hopes on Him who saith,
"Unto the least," the outcast poor,
Who, hungering wait beside your door,
But do the deeds He would have done,
And say to every starving one:
      "Dinner!"

REACH ME YOUR HAND.

Reach me your hand, down from the heights serene,
  Where you today secure and smiling stand;
While winds blow cold and night comes o'er the scene,
Through shadows dark and yawning gulf between—
  Reach me your hand.

Reach me your hand, when hope is almost gone;
  I've wandered far across life's desert sand,
But now to see you in the glorious dawn
Away to turn, and sadly journey on—
  Reach me your hand.

Reach me your hand, I cannot wander far,
  For here the light is flooding all the land;
While otherwhere the deepening shadows are,
And hopeless night, a night without a star,
  Reach me your hand.

Reach me your hand, I will not go away,
  I'll climb the heights my longing eyes have scanned,
No more through rough and devious paths to stray,
And while we wait to greet the coming day
  Reach me your hand.

REACH ME YOUR HAND.

Reach me your hand, the light is come at last,
 The hills of morn, by freshening breezes fanned,
Rejoice together. Night and gloom are past,
Behold the day! The day is coming fast—
 Reach me your hand.

SPRING ON SANTA CATALINA.

The winter passed with wind and rain,
   And fitful scenes of shade and light.
The mists came drifting off the main,
And loud I heard the waves complain
   Upon the lonely shore at night.

Full oft I watched the flying bark
   That labored through the crested waves,
When night was falling drear and dark,
With not a star or light to mark
   Where yawned the sailors' watery graves.

And ere the dawn of one sad day,
   I know the spot, upon the reef,
Where, in the rocks and dashing spray
By treacherous currents borne away,
   The good ship struck, and came to grief.

The cruel waves upon her cast
   A crushing weight of waters then;
The cruel rocks, they held her fast,
Away went shroud and spar and mast
   And clinging forms of drowning men.

*   *   *   *

SPRING ON SANTA CATALINA.

Another picture comes the while;
  The sun returns to cheer and bless,
The tempest stilled, the waters smile,
And over all th' enchanted isle
  The flowers feel the spring's caress.

And bursting forth in beauty rare
  A wealth of golden poppies spread,
As if the sunbeams, passing fair,
Were well content to linger there
  Upon each floweret's modest head.

And all the sounds that come to me
  Are call of quail from canyon lone,
The waters murmuring toward the sea,
The whispering breeze within the tree,
  And lapse of wave o'er shell and stone.

Oh, fairer than a poet's dream,
  The flowering land, the flowing sea!
For brighter skies could never beam,
And brighter waves could never gleam
  Upon the sands, eternally.

OUR CASTLE IN SPAIN.

In the glorious time of our youthful prime
    When unknown was the shadow of pain,
And the world was ours with its birds and flowers
    We builded our castle in Spain.
The walls they were jasper, the towers were gold,
    The windows looked over the sea;
But alas! Those windows are dark and cold,
    And cold and dark shall they be.

No fire is alight on the hearth at night,
    No music is heard in the hall,
While the spectral trees as they sway in the breeze
    Are tapping at window and wall;
And bleak desolation is reigning supreme
    Where gladness did only abide,
For no one can live in this place it would seem
    Since the lord of the castle has died.

Yes, I died long ago in the night of my woe
    When they bore a young bride from the door,
And my body with her's is at rest 'neath the firs
    On the cliff by the storm-beaten shore.
But at night when the moon, rising over the glen,
    Looks in at the desolate pane
There are strange sights and sounds, for we wander again
    Through the halls of our castle in Spain.

NINETEEN HUNDRED.

Nineteen hundred, magic spell,
I can read thy meaning well;
I can see or seem to see
All the fate that waits for thee,
And my heart, though strong and brave,
Falters that I may not save
Friends and brothers true and leal
From the conflict and ordeal.

But thy horoscope is clear,
Year of fate and fateful year.
We have waited long for thee,
Crowning year of destiny.
We have seen thy star arise
Like a promise through the skies,
And our hearts expectant beat
Till thy reign shall be complete.

Ere we see thy dawning day
Thrones may pass in fire away
Ermine robe and golden crown
In the dust be trampled down.
All its useless hoard of gold
Wealth with trembling hands shall hold,
Crouching in its gilded home,
Lo! the judgment day is come.

Gold! accursed of tongue and pen;
Gold! despair of toiling men;
Gold! the power behind the throne,
Gold is evil, gold alone.
Haste the day when gold shall be
Banished with plutocracy!
Year of fate and fateful year,
Nineteen Hundred draweth near.

FROM MY SCRAP-BOOK.

Come with me apart from the maddening throng
   And cool in the soft summer twilight recline,
While I read you my treasures of poetry and song
   That I've hoarded for years in this scrap-book of mine.
They are culled as the choicest and fairest of flowers
   That have bloomed by the side of my wearisome way,
And the comfort and solace of many lone hours
   Do I owe to the gems that I bring you today.

They will whisper of hope when the future looks dreary
   And deep are the shadows that darken your way;
They will tell you of rest when the spirit is weary,
   Oppressed by the burden and heat of the day.
So, great is my treasure and fain would I share it,
   'Twill make it not less to divide it with you;
No burden so heavy but that we may bear it
   When comforted, strengthened and girded anew.

Here's a story of love, 'tis so touching and tender
   I fear if I read it your eyes will o'erflow,
And yet, all the wealth of its beauty and splendor,
   And feeling sublime. I would have you to know.
But if, in the reading, when utterance fail me,
   I come to an end ere the story be through,
As the strong tides of feeling rise up and assail me,
   You'll call me not weak and unworthy of you.

For the story I read is the one that has trembled
  Full oft on my lips in the days that have passed;
But I feared I would shatter the dream, and dissembled,
  And sought to conceal it from you to the last.
But tenderly, sweetly, the words of the poet
  Have opened the portal to feelings divine,
And you understand, for your beaming eyes show it,
  And thankful am I for this scrap-book of mine.

THE ANGEL'S VISIT.

In our chamber, scant and meager,
  Lay my friend; I watched beside,
Waiting patiently, yet eager
  For the turn of life's low tide.
Midnight came, no sound or motion
  In the dim, uncertain light:
Would this bark on life's broad ocean
  Reach its port this fateful night?

Oh, the thought my spirit maddened!
  All my life were chaos then,
Only bittered, crushed and saddened
  By the dreams of what had been.
Up I sprang with imprecations—
  Threw my window open wide,
There to still my brow's pulsations
  In the night's all-healing tide.

Pitying skies were bending o'er me,
  Faithful stars their vigils kept,
Wide the world outspread before me
  Where the weary mortals slept.
Ah, but hark! a sound appealing,
  From a mansion lone and far,
On the waves of silence stealing
  Notes of viol and guitar.

THE ANGEL'S VISIT.

From the halls of wealth and splendor
    Came those melodies divine,
Touched my soul with pathos tender
    In that poor retreat of mine.
And I said, "O, angel, brooding
    O'er this couch I hold so dear,
Enter not, thy form intruding,
    Come not near! oh, come not near!"

But my prayer was unavailing,
    For within my humble room,
Robed in garments dark and trailing,
    Moved a Shape of stately gloom;
Waved its hand and beckoned to me,
    I could choose not but obey;
With a subt power it drew me
    And I questioned not the way.

Silently, to my amazement,
    This dark presence guiding me,
Out we floated through the casement,
    Toward the halls of revelry.
With the merry dancers speeding
    Through the mazes, in and out,
They unknowing or unheeding
    That we joined the festive rout.

" Let not care and sorrow darkle
    Hearts that burn with youth's bright fires,
Lips that smile and eyes that sparkle,
    Breasts that heave with love's desires.

THE ANGEL'S VISIT.

Gloom and sadness leave till morrow,
    Banish grief with tuneful tread;
Joy is fleeting, grasp it; sorrow
    Lingers when all else is fled.

So we wound the dreamy measures
    While the viols sobbed and wept,
Till, despite those fleeting pleasures,
    In my heart a horror crept!
Then the vision from me flitting,
    Left me in the morning chill;
By my window I was sitting
    With my head upon the sill.

Sudden fear my heart appalling,
    Up I started from the spot;
By the bedside kneeling, calling
    To the form that answered not.
Nothing more the pale lips uttered,
    Stilled for aye the faltering breath,
For the soul had outward fluttered
    On the sable wings of Death.

Go, little book, with right good will,
    Upon thine errand sent;
May God forbid thou bearest ill
    Where only good is meant.

To render less the load of care,
    The weight of human woe,
To whisper hope to wan despair,—
    For this I bid thee go.

And if thou brought some sweet return
    Of kindly thought or deed,
If friendship's fires should brighter burn,
    Oh! that were blest indeed.